Part One: Inside Job

Chapter 1: Patience is a virtue

I was standing there waiting for the bank teller to wait on me and there were seven other people ahead of me. I was patiently waiting in line like any of these people were supposed to. Normal, yeah ha-ha I hate that word and it equates to something different to other people. It is a recipe of disaster to think that your needs are more important than other peoples.

Who is truly normal? I really didn't want to keep letting that question pester me. I was as patient as the next person, but this line was extremely long. Confucius needed to be strangled for saying the quote "patience is a virtue" because that is a huge lie. I'm surprised this line wasn't out the door by now!

All these people must be wasting their lunch trying to get their banking I thought. It must be nice to have an extended lunch like I do. With the time it would take to get through to all these people. I could have ate a sandwich and chugged a soda while waiting. There was at least ten people or so and only two tellers were on duty. The other three tellers that are usually on must have been on lunch too. I tended to get easily distracted when I waited in her line. My mind tended to drift, just like it is now.

I began daydreaming and my thoughts running wild. As I canvassed the place I realized it really wasn't all that secure. What if this bank were to have a robbery right now? Just a hypothetical question. Who doesn't think about that when waiting in line at a bank or a store? I know I do! The guard who was on duty was in

no shape to capture any perpetrators. He was

quite the husky guy with snow white wiry hair

and it looked like it was thinning. His hair

reminded me of Grandpa Munster. He was short,

probably no taller than 5'5. He had dark blue

pants with a belt that looked like a size too

small. His stomach slightly bulged out, revealing

his white undershirt. It wasn't hard to see that

shirt he didn't wear a tie. It was comical because

he looked tired like he just chased a suspect and

and chugged a soda while waiting. There was at least ten people or so and only two tellers were on duty. The other three tellers that are usually on must have been on lunch too. I tended to get easily distracted when I waited in her line. My mind tended to drift, just like it is now.

I began daydreaming and my thoughts running wild. As I canvassed the place I realized it really wasn't all that secure. What if this bank were to have a robbery right now? Just a hypothetical question. Who doesn't think about that when waiting in line at a bank or a store? I know I do! The guard who was on duty was in no shape to capture any perpetrators. He was quite the husky guy with snow white wiry hair and it looked like it was thinning. His hair reminded me of Grandpa Munster. He was short, probably no taller than 5'5. He had dark blue pants with a belt that looked like a size too small. His stomach slightly bulged out, revealing his white undershirt. It wasn't hard to see that shirt he didn't wear a tie. It was comical because he looked tired like he just chased a suspect and already needed a nap. The guard's name is Frank according to the name on his badge.

The bank teller I was waiting to assist me had helped me many times before. Her name is Alex, and she is jaw dropping gorgeous. She is the type of woman you see as a model or on a soap opera. There were no other words could describe her but that. She was probably way out of my league, but that didn't mean I didn't always try to smooth talk her. Great, now comes the negative self talk that lingers through my mind. She may have been out of my league, but that didn't bother me. i was game enough to play her fucked up chess game.

Alex has long flowing red hair and cream colored skin. She didn't look like she visited a tanning booth at all. That didn't matter to me though, she has a subtle amount of freckles and she always put on a fake smile. She enticed me more than anyone could dream of. I would go through her line purposely every time I came to the bank. I didn't care about the wait and I much rather enjoyed the intrinsic reward. I imagined her hair and skin were silky smooth and smelled like peaches and vanilla. I would love nothing more than to run my fingers through her hair.

Her body was more of a voluptuous figure, but I was a man who enjoyed curves. She blushed at the slightest things and she was so adorable when she did. She always blushed and smiled when she saw me. She has a voice that could make you melt and she has a slightly nasal giggle. She was much to be desired for, and yet I was afraid to make a move.

Guys liked to flirt with her or make advances at her quite often. She always turned them away with a kind smile. She always made time for me and flirted back with me though.

I think I just lacked the confidence and so I just didn't want to make the effort. She is a particularly high maintenance woman. She probably didn't date guys like me. She would probably laugh at me if i were mention the word date.

I work as Cyber Security Specialist and I took care of any cyber attacks that may intrude websites and mobile apps. I could hack the hell out of anything, but I decided to work this job as

as a cover.

I had done a lot of bad shit in my past and

made millions of dollars doing it. I would do it

again without a care in the world too. I was what

they called a black hat hacker. I knew how to

hack into private accounts and syphon their cash.

I didn't do any illegal things while I was at

work, but all bets were off when I was off the

clock. I have made software, hacked people, sold

counterfeit software, made viruses and made

money off get rich sites. I have done a lot of bad

shit I'm not proud of. These jobs were necessary

though. If only there was a massive group of

other hackers who all believed in the cause. I

feel no remorse for doing any of it either. A lot

of my clients come from old money

       I could probably clean this bank out in an

hour or less if their security wasn't up to par.

They had multiple cameras, security switches

under each cashiers desk. If there was any

problems they could have cops there in 2-3

minutes. It would take some surveillance and a

few weeks of preparation, but I could do it. Now

out of anything, but I decided to work this job as

as a cover.

I had done a lot of bad shit in my past and

made millions of dollars doing it. I would do it

again without a care in the world too. I was what

they called a black hat hacker. I knew how to

hack into private accounts and syphon their cash.

I didn't do any illegal things while I was at

work, but all bets were off when I was off the

clock. I have made software, hacked people, sold

counterfeit software, made viruses and made

money off get rich sites. I have done a lot of bad

shit I'm not proud of. These jobs were necessary

though. If only there was a massive group of

other hackers who all believed in the cause. I

feel no remorse for doing any of it either. A lot

of my clients come from old money

        I could probably clean this bank out in an

hour or less if their security wasn't up to par.

They had multiple cameras, security switches

under each cashiers desk. If there was any

problems they could have cops there in 2-3

minutes. It would take some surveillance and a

few weeks of preparation, but I could do it. Now

the only way to do this is to befriend my teller friend. I have shut off all security in a bank or casino in the past via remote access. It's easier to do than have a group of people come in and strong arme place. I wondered what was behind the vault. It would be great to see cash, gold, rare coins, bonds, and other valuables.

As I was standing in line some douchebag pushed in front of me. He thought it was ok to be rude to Alex. She wasn't paid enough to put up with this shit.

"What the fuck is taking so long? Don't

these tellers know what the hell they're doing? A

trained monkey could go faster!" said the

douchebag who was just ahead of me.

I guess the asshole was on lunch break or

he was trying to deposit money for his company.

Maybe he was trying to get a loan or some

stupid shit like that. The loan officer was on

lunch, if so he might want to come back. Who

the hell cares and really I don't want to think

about it further.

Maybe I could beat the hell out of him and he

would never disrespect anyone again. Why is

that you might ask? That is because he would hit

rock bottom and he would probably end up

bankrupt.

I could lift his wallet and I could switch

out his identity with a stolen identity and some

counterfeit bills. I could take his envelope of

money and switch it with counterfeit money.

That one might be a little harder. I could do a

lot of devious and destructive things. I had been

a pickpocket before in my past and that was how

I made my living. How do you think magicians and street performers make a living? It's pretty easy to deceive some people because some people are gullible and naïve. It's all about the illusion that makes something appear or disappear. It's sleight of hand that makes the trick so good. I could switch out wallets with him without a problem. It's all about respect and he needs to respect people. Those bank tellers work too damn hard for little of nothing. I really hope this guy goes to get a loan. That would give me ample time. I think he was getting a loan or setting up a new account. I wish I didn't

overthink things and ramble so much. My head

can't take it.

"Next please. Silas pay attention you're

next" said Alex.

"Oh sorry, really I am" I said.

"How can I help you today and for God sake

friggin' smile will you" said Alex

jokingly.

"I need to open a CD account" I said excitedly.

"Oh wow a certificate of deposit. That's huge!"

she said in shock.

If she only knew where I got the money

she would be even more shocked, but I am not

going to say anything to her unless I can trust

her. I could tell a back story about how It was an

inheritance or that I won a good hand of poker.

Right, let's go with the poker. I'm smart I could

probably pass for someone who counts cards.

What the hell does she know anyways?

Seriously and why does it really matter? I got

the money from robbing a bank online. I told

you that I was an IT security guy, but it doesn't

pay much. I get thirty-five grand a year and I get

bonuses of one thousand dollars every three months, but that is only when the company does really well.

"I would like to deposit 50 thousand dollars" I said with a cocky smile.

"Sure I can do that" said Alex with her own grin. She whispers to me really quietly "Where did you get this kind of money?" She was really curious and I had to make up something. No one was around so I made up something believable.

"I won a few good hands of poker. This is only a small amount of what I won." I whispered happily. "I can count cards too, but I sure as hell

don't do that too often because I don't feel like

getting my hands broke or wearing concrete

shoes" I said with a little humor.

"Well I would be careful what you spend and

what you invest, it's still taxable income" she

said with hesitation. "You don't want the IRS

wondering where the hell you got 50k"

"That's where you come in! I would like to put it

in my nephew's name like it's a college fund" I

said with a sly grin.

"I'm not sure if I can do that, but I can sure as hell try. I think you would have to put it in his mother's name and she would have to come in and do it for him" she said swiftly. "I'm only following protocol and trying to cover my ass" she said with a little bit of hesitation.

"My nephew lives with me and I have all of his info" I said quickly, as I tried to answer her questions with ease.

The thing about banks, when you wave money around they will happily take a large amount and break rules, that's if you're doing it as a charitable action. My nephew Brian did live with me and he is 12 years old. I have full custody because his mother is a painkiller addict and an alcoholic. Opening accounts in his name at multiple banks was easy and he couldn't touch any of it until 18 or older. This was money for him, as well as for the both of us. This was money we saved to tell the bank screw off. I earned it by doing random hack jobs off the books. This money would mature and interest would build and it would be untraceable.

I enjoyed the fact that I was setting up a retirement fund and a college fund for my nephew. This way his ass could go to Harvard or MIT. I wasn't going to let him flip burgers or go to some community college. We were going to have money for a long time or for the rest of our lives. We would live like kings and no one would stop us. I didn't mind doing what I did because honestly I wasn't afraid of getting caught. Who's going to catch us the FBI or CIA? Whenever they try to catch us we will escape extradition. We will move somewhere else out

of reach and become ghosts.

It was actually pretty easy to trick the

banks and I could transfer the money to another

country or Bitcoin. Banks are quite ignorant

when you wave money at them like a carrot to a

donkey. I had been doing it for years and so had

my partners. Opening savings accounts, CD's,

business accounts, getting loans for large items.

We were unstoppable!

I did the positive computer work for

people by day at ClearNet and helped businesses

avoid attacks. While on my off time I did black hat or gray hat hacking. I did it for all the wealthy customers who could afford to spy on other sites. Not only did I do that, but I hacked some of those same large corporations, banks, and casinos. I found ways to infiltrate their security or we outright robbed them with guns, anonymous masks and black hoodies. We wore bullet proof vests underneath and we were invincible. We had nothing to lose and everything to gain. We robbed their stupid asses' blind! We never got caught whether it was a hack job or a robbery. It was hilarious and the

money we made was astronomical!

A month ago we did a heist and got away

with a little over one million dollars. Splitting it

among four people that's over a quarter million

each. That's actually quite a good payday.

That's a better payday than my own yearly wage

and I'm dumbfounded by how easy it is. I had to

find a way to hide the money, so what a better

way than to let the money sit for a while. Before

I tell you more about my other big scores and

what I do; I probably should tell you more about

my past.

Chapter 2: Welcome to Paradise

It all started when I was a teenager and I was just trying to find a way to make ends meet. I was 13 years old and my parents were dirt poor. We did still have a decent amount of things coming in and out of the house though. I remember that we didn't have an up to date computer until I was 11 or 12. I was able to take apart and put together computers and other small electronics by the age of 8. Electronics

fascinated me and they fascinated my dad too.
That was the only thing he was really good at
and the only thing we shared in common. I
actually went on to learn about electronics and
learn about computers. My mind was like a
sponge and I retained all of this knowledge
because I enjoyed learning about small
electronics and computers. My parents finally
did get a decent computer when I was a junior in
high school. When I learned about computers
and small electronics at a technical school in
high school I was always fixing their computer

and other frivolous junk. I learned quite quickly

how to fix viruses, how to spot one, and how to

maximize the computer to its full potential.

For my birthday, when I was a senior in

high school, my parents got me my own laptop. I

was so ecstatic to have this because now I could

do things I was taught on my own. I decided to

stay after school and learn more about the

technical side of computers with my instructor

Mr. Livingston. He taught me how to create a

virus, how to create software, and he taught me

the basics of white hat and black hat hacking. He

taught me a lot of other tips and tricks like

pirating expensive software and how to use my

computer to its full capacity and how to watch

TV online without cable tv. The guy was an

absolute computer genius and he could do just

about anything. He knew more about the internet

world and computer world than I could ever

imagine knowing. Hacking became something I

decided to learn on my own and from a

collective community of others online. I literally

developed skills beyond my years and I was the

go to person for all of the answers. The only

problem was I was leaving a breadcrumb trail

leading back to me. My hacking and pirating

were starting to catch back up to me.

I was doing a multitude of things that I

shouldn't have been doing. I hacked the school

records department and changed my grades. I

hacked a college university I sent an application

to. I put my name in their system for an

acceptance letter. I pirated expensive software

that costed hundreds of dollars per software. I

felt like I was God and I felt invincible. I even

sent a virus via email with an anonymous email.

It infected a bunch of people's computers. I marked it as a free sample in exchange for an email. You would not believe how many people clicked the link. The link turned their computer into a slave and any time they entered personal information it was sent to my computer.

I talked to my instructor about the different things I did and he told me I had to completely wipe my computer and do it fast. He gave me a software called Disk Wipe and told me to completely wipe all my computers and restore all regular programs to make it look natural. Put all the programs and files I wanted to save on an external hard drive first. He told me to leave no trace of what happened. He told me to lie low and use a public computer at the library or at a cyber café. I could also use my own stuff like a portable cellphone or tablet with a portable hotspot, but avoid free Wi-Fi unless it was the libraries or cafes. His pearls of wisdom really helped me.

I was glad that he did give me the software because a week later a detective named Detective Thurston. He came to see me and ask a few questions about a case the FBI was working on. I was extremely nervous about the visit, but there was nothing I could really do about it. They were on to me and I hoped they would find nothing. What was I nervous about though? As long as I did the wipe right, so there should be no issues.

"Are you Silas Baker" the detective said sternly.

"Yes I am. And who are you?" I said prodding at him. I really wasn't in the mood for bullshit from some idiot in a cheap suit.

"I'm Detective John Thurston and this is my

assistant Detective Frank Gray. I was just

wondering if we could have a word with you" he

said inquisitively.

He had a warrant and the other detective

was a forensic computer analyst.

He wanted to look at my laptop and my parents

desktop. The only problem is he didn't have a

warrant to search the entire premises. I had

another laptop I bought with my own money and

I had my cellphone in my room. The laptop was

cleaned out too. I was glad that they had no

authority to anything else and of course they

found nothing because the one computer. That

was my parents computer. Mine was cleaned out

and I hid the software somewhere safe.. I was in

the clear, at least for now I was. For all they

knew, it could have been someone else using a

computer's WiFi or an electronic device in the

area that had hacked my Wi-Fi.

"I may not have anything on you now right now

punk! We'll meet again you little prick and I'll

be the one to catch you" said detective Thurston.

With that he left with his dignity intact, or at

least I hope he still had some dignity. After

being embarrassed like that, he probably didn't.

Chapter 3: Attack From Within

I sat there at my computer trying to plot

my next hack. I was searching for a guy named

Alejandro Rejos. He was a high level drug seller

on the deep web. He sold on a .onion site called

The Silk Road. It was the E-bay or Amazon of

the drug world.

You may be listening to me and wonder

what the Deep Web is. So let me educate you

briefly how the internet works. Say, you want a piece of pie and the internet is pie. The internet or all the popular sites as you know it is a very little piece of pie. It takes months for a site to get properly indexed and years to get seen by "millions". The movie *Field of Dreams* lied. Just because someone builds it or creates it does not mean people will magically come. A blog, Facebook page, personal web page, and forum are better ways for people to find you. They will make more money and generate residual income.

There are hundreds or even thousands of new websites being built and indexed each day and that many more disappear into cyberspace never to be seen again. Maybe 1% to 20% of what you find on the internet is not really the only thing that's out there. The search engines, especially Google, keep websites from being available from sight unless their PR or page rank is high and their organic traffic is high. Now that I explained that let's explain .onion sites and worldwide traffic sites or sites located in countries with no

U.S. authority. Some of these examples include:

.se, .la, .to, .be, and .gs and other weird

extensions are usually used for private sites.

Places like pirating sites, blogs, forums, and

underground sites. These people rely strictly on

donations through direct pay sites.

Now to access the .onion site you need to

use a free program called TOR. Which is a

search engine to surf the Deep Web. Now that I

explained all of this to you, let me explain how

I'm tracking this mother fucker. Now of course I

had to use Tor to access this site. These sites

were supposed to be hidden from the general

public and government agencies. Of course sites

like The Silk Road were known by the public

because of TV, blogs, articles, and other media.

The government is not as daft ad you may think

either. They had hackers and computer experts

on their own staff to help them. The people on

some of these underground sites were just as

smart as them or smarter than some of those paid

agents. I wish I could have been one of them, but

of course they didn't think I was qualified.

Maybe someday they would regret that decision

of not allowing me to work with them.

Ok now back to reality and back to the

task at hand. I needed to chase down this scum

before he caused any more problems on the web.

He was a high level seller of opiates and people

enjoyed ordered from him. He was selling drugs

to teens and he was also ordering hits on other

dealers. Some of these other dealers

were only selling just like he was and they were

doing it comfortably from their own home. They

had families and friends and they didn't deserve

to be killed by him because he wanted to be a

drug kingpin of The Silk Road I didn't want to

just close down his site, I wanted to do more

than that. I wanted vigilante justice. I doubt that

would happen, but it was worth a try.

I finally found him after searching for at

least 20 minutes and multiple profiles. I found

him and I placed an order, but with that order I

posted a small file in the comments section. It

was titled "open for more details" because who

could avoid looking at the details. I also was

able to get his email address and sent him a file

from an anonymous dummy email and it said "earn the wealth of your dreams". If he opened either one of them his computer would be rendered useless. I even sent something to his phone via text from a burner phone. It was a text message attachment for a video and it would reduce his phone to nothing more than a brick. Hopefully he would answer. I also geo-located where he was and I will scope him out for a while. It will be a matter of time before I am able to take him down one way or another and if not I will kill him.

I was finally able to find him and I tracked

him to somewhere a few cities away from me in

Ventura, California. I made up a quick dummy

Wi-Fi connection with my hotspot and named

Starbucks Ventura ave. I knew that he would

click on

it and so would a lot of others. He was in line

ordering coffee at a small café. He sat down and

he must have clicked on my open network that I

had set up because I noticed a computer by the

name of Ar3j0s trying to sign on to my network.

I cannot believe he fell for this trap. I would be

able to access all of his files and send him a

virus now. I send him a terms and conditions

document with something attached. He agreed

and now it was time for the magic to happen.

The attachment installed a ransomware virus on

his computer. This would cause him some issues

for a while. I even had it set up where as soon as

he opened up the computer at home any device

he used would be infected. So of course if he

didn't get the files I sent him before he would

now be infected. I set the ransom at $50,000 and

I made it almost impossible to remove. He

would even infect his phone and any other device if he shared files. I liked that I finally had got one scumbag off the web. Now all I had to see was if he was going to pay the ransom.

Chapter 4: I got 99 problems

It was Thursday morning and it was 9:00 am. I had to go to work and deal with the daily grind of computer work as an IT specialist. My job was to ensure that websites and software weren't vulnerable of attacks. I was able to find issues with people's sites before anyone else could. I was the person that clients and other specialists turned to when they needed help.

Some people knew just how good my abilities

were and how advanced I was. I was actually

younger than most people who worked there,

and at the age of 23, I was ruthlessly moving

myself up the ranks. Many people I worked

alongside were dumbfounded by my real

abilities and true potential. I was more advanced

than anyone that I worked with and I'm

surprised no one was envious of me. I kept

records of who I helped and I kept it for my own

reference later. What did you think I would do just erase it?

Finally, it was time to go home after a long day of helping large companies like Target, Walmart, and other places keep their sites safe. I had to get home to see my nephew Damien and relieve the babysitter of her servitude. Little did some of these sites know that I would be attacking them again later!

It had been about a week since I had seen Alex. I went to deposit some more money into my savings account, but my excuse was to see her. So I drove over there and I got there like a

half an hour before it closed. The smile on her

face

could tell a thousand stories.

"Hi Silas good to see you again" said Alex with

a big smile.

"Ya I'm sure you're happy to see me again" said

Silas with a grin and smooth confidence.

"What do you need today?" said Alex smiling

politely.

"Well I need to make a deposit of $10,000 into

my nephew's savings account and I also would

like your phone number" Silas said smoothly.

"Ok let me deposit that for you really quick and

done. Ooooh and for once you're being a cocky

and confident man I like it. You see, you talk a

nice talk, but I sense something white collar or

shady beyond the nephew and the IT specialist

job. You'll have to do more than just talk a big

game. My bosses may like you, and you and

your nephew are so damn cute, but you need to

lay it on thick with me" said Alex sweetly and

with a little humor. She handed me her number though on a piece receipt paper and she was so sweet doing it too. She even left a little heart at the bottom.

"Just call me later we can have dinner together or something" I said without a care in the world.

I may have been afraid before, but I wasn't now.

"Ok cowboy we'll see. I'll get back to you on that" she said coyly with a smile.

"I'll even teach you about some of the boring work that I do" I said with sarcasm.

And there it was, the word vomit, my mouth

says something it shouldn't more often than not.

I definitely shouldn't have said anything because

now of course she's going to want to know

more.

"Oh ya…what do you do Silas?" Alex asked

nicely.

"I am an IT specialist for a company who

prevents big companies from being hacked of

course. I keep out the bad guys. I also help

private clients too"

"When you say you keep out the bad guys, that means at one time you must have done hacking and some other bad stuff too?" Alex asked in a prodding way like she was trying to pull an alligator tooth.

"There was a time when I did it yes and that was a much darker time, a much darker Silas" I said trying to sound convincing. Even I wanted to believe that.

Alex seemed gullible enough and she acted like she was head over heels for me. "I think we should go take a walk after you finish up. I can talk more after. Maybe I can teach you a few

things"

"Ok deal I get done in 10 minutes. Go wait

outside now I have to close up."

I had never felt so aroused before than I did

when she bossed me around. She was hot when

she was bossy and I wanted to be bossed around

some more. Give it time though and it would

happen again. I sat outside of the bank, inside of

my air conditioned car, listening to Metallica as

I come waited for her to get done and

lock up. Someday soon though I would figure out what the combination to the bank vault was and what the code to the alarm system was. I would make sure that I was able to rob this bank like the many other places I have robbed around the city. All I needed to do was befriend Alex and I was good as golden.

"Oh there you are I'm glad you waited. So let's ride up to the park and we'll talk there. How does that sound?" Alex said with a chipper voice.

"Sure. That sounds great. I'll follow your car

there. Let's go now. My babysitter can work

overtime. She gets paid pretty well. I'll call her

when I get up to the park" I said with vigor.

"Ok let's see if you can keep up. Follow the

silver Acura. I drive pretty fast" she said

flirtatiously.

"I'll do my best" he said.

I followed her in my red 69 Ford Mustang and I

was surprised how fast she was able to go in that

junky Acura. I wasn't into the newer cars. Older

model cars were my forte. I could boost them up

and make them shine like a newer car. I had a

really loud engine though so I had to go the

speed limit and not rev up the engine. The

spoilers are supposed to make me go faster and

reduce drag, but I think all of my enhancement

make the car sexy, but the engine run like shit. I

guess I'll get there when I get there. She stopped

at a Valero gas station and I was confused as

to why.

"Hey let's stop and get a drink" she said with a

smile.

She bought a few 20 oz. cans of Budweiser

Strawberita's and we drove to the park.

Glad you could make it. Now let's talk about

what it is that you do" she said with a smile.

I could tell this was going to be

interesting. I wasn't going to lie, but I was going

to have to sell this story like my life depended

on it. I needed a partner and a fall woman and

she was the perfect candidate.

Chapter 5: Glimpse in time

I still remember the time that I had issues

with Detective Thurston. He was always on my

tail. He constantly followed me and he

constantly monitored me. Somehow he got a

hold of one of my e-mails and he was sending

me messages all the time. I even reported him to

his chief and they did nothing. He ran the

cybercrime and white collar crime divisions and

they weren't concerned with his actions. I still

filed a report with his seniors and filed for an

order of protection against him. It felt good that

it was quiet, but it was a little too quiet. I feared

that maybe I pissed off the wrong guy. Maybe I

had to give him a dose of bad medicine. I would

not be proud of what I did next, but I had to do

it, it was for my own good. I would have to

blackmail detective Thurston or else he would

build a case against me. I wasn't the type to take

kindly to going to jail, so I had to out think

Detective Thurston.

I messed with the city police department

database for a few days and then I was finally

able to hack in as Detective Thurston. I made it

look like he had finally gone dirty. I made it

look like he was hiding evidence in a series of

his white collar investigations and made it look

like he was embezzling money. I even created

fake incriminating documents and sent them

anonymously to the chief of police. This wasn't

the only thing that I was going to do. Not by a

long shot! I got a hold of his

private work email and I hacked into it. I sent

messages to everyone on the force with a video

attached. In the video I was wearing an

anonymous mask and showing cue cards with

written messages. The basic message said not to

trust Detective Thurston. I told them that he had

cleaned out everyone's 401k and retirement fund

and deposited it in the Cayman Islands. I did just

that too. I wiped out every police officer's 401k

and retirement pension but 2 people. One of

them was Detective Thurston and of course he

had to have a fall guy. Why not make it

Detective Gray? He's the dumb one of the bunch

he'll never expect it at all.

Chapter 6: Word Vomit

As we sat watching the sunset I was trying

to decide what I was going to say. If I lied it

would have to be a really good lie. It would have

to be the best lie I told in my life. My mom

always told me that a lie only leads to more lies,

thus creating an avalanche of lies. I lived my life

based on a lie though. No one really knew what I

actually did except for very few people. No one

actually understood me. My psychologist didn't

even understand me and sometimes I sat there

hardly talking. Each session was a wasted

session and there seemed to be no progress. I

was diagnosed with multiple disorders.

Schizophrenia, anxiety, depression. I was a

textbook case for the all-around nut case. I

hoped that Alex wouldn't see that.

"Ok so you want to know more about me? I'm

not sure where I should start? I work as a

technical support specialist during the day. I am

similar to a white hat hacker. I keep out all of the

bad hackers and I test securities and

vulnerabilities. How do I know about this?

Because on my off time I am a black hat hacker.

I actually can hack just about anything with no

problem" I said arrogantly

And there was the word vomit I was

referring to. I sounded like such an asshole when

I was talking about this. I said it so nonchalantly

and I wasn't even drunk or buzzed. She looked

at me puzzled me like she thought I was joking.

I wasn't joking in the least. I had been doing

hacking for a long while now. I had

been looking for someone to join my inner circle

and I wondered if I could trust her. I think it was

also because I liked her. My friend Seth, a

fellow hacker, said I should never let pussy

distract me, but she was just seemed different

than the rest. I trusted her more than I trusted the

rest of the women I dated. I haven't even asked

her out yet, but I had been going to her bank a

long time now and she has been pulling strings

for me. That had to mean something!

"Do you think you could hack into somewhere like my bank?" she said curiously.

I was so thrown back by that question. I wasn't even going to ask about something like this for a while. I would have befriended her for a long time before I asked. I almost didn't want to respond.

"You're kidding right? Yes I probably could in 5 to 10 minutes with the right passwords or the right clearance. If I didn't I could still hack it in 20 minutes or less. Why are you asking?"

"Oh no reason. I do know that my bank is going to acquire millions in art, gems, coins, and other priceless items. I know that the vault will be acquiring a new code and they will be ramping up their security. They have a lot of camera blind spots and security loopholes though" she said very convincingly. Either she was buzzed after a few drinks or she was just intrigued in trying to get involved in my life of crime. Either way I liked this side of her and I wanted to see more of it.

I really liked this evil side of her and was more

interested in her then ever. I hope she wasn't

pulling my leg or was one of those ones who

talked only when they were drunk. I really didn't

want to have to get her drunk or high every time

I wanted to make a big score.

"I'm interested in this more than you can even

imagine and I would love to make you part of

my crew Alex" I said excitedly.

"Really! You mean it? I could make an excellent

crew member. I could be a great mole and I

could also be a great distraction. I would love to

learn what you know. If you're willing to teach

me that is" she said with enthusiasm.

I had never taught anyone from the basics on up.

This might be hard, but maybe she would be a

quick learner. I hoped she would be a quick

learner. I could use her to infiltrate this bank.

She was a trusted member of her bank. She was

a head bank manager or head bank teller. She

knew the ins and outs of that bank. She knew

just as much or more about it than her own boss.

She was there more than the top executives.

"I will start teaching you tomorrow. I will give

you an initiation job tomorrow. Until then I need

to get home to my nephew" I said slyly.

She gave me a goodnight kiss and we both left. I

was so happy to know that our date ended with a

kiss and a promising possibility of more. This

was more than I

expected and much more than she probably

expected too.

I drove home and finally relieved the babysitter

of her duties. It was 9:00 at night and my

nephew was so glad to see me. He would be

going to bed soon, but I really was glad to be home.

"Uncle Silas! You're home! How was your date?" Brian said he said sarcastically.

I could see that he was happy to see me. The glee on his face told the story. I don't think he liked his babysitter Tiffany. I think she was just in it for the money. As much as she loved watching him I don't think she enjoyed the extra hours sometimes. She enjoyed the extra pay she got and believe me I paid her really well! She happily left and I got Brian ready for bed. He brushed his teeth, put on something for bed, and

he got in bed. I put on his radio and he fell

asleep almost immediately. He is an easy sleeper

and that is very comforting to me. The rest of the

night was mine to prepare for my next jobs and

to go to sleep myself. That in itself can be hard

because my mind is always wandering. Now I

also had to worry about my new friend Alex. I

hoped that I wasn't in over my head with her and

I hoped that I really didn't become too interested

in her.

Chapter 7: Never give up

Detective Thurston sat at his desk reading the morning paper about a person who had made money as a freelance computer specialist at home. He read how this person tested company's websites for vulnerabilities. He knew that this was a crock of shit. The person's name was Randall Franklin. He had many run ins with Franklin, just like he did with Silas. Randall and Silas almost cost him his job when they did antics involving insider trading, insurance fraud, and embezzling of retirement funds. If he didn't recoup the funds and fix the situation he would have been fired. He wondered how Randall was and he felt like harassing him for any illegal things he might be doing now.

Chapter 8: No Chance

I sat there meditating as I tried to reach my chi for the day. I sat there in silence almost asleep as my cell phone alarm went off. The shrill of the alarm kept getting louder and louder until I finally pressed quit. I finally felt balanced and centered for the day, that was until a video message popped up on my

screen. It was his friend Randall.

"Dude, that scumbag Thurston is trying to shake us down again. He's trying to build a case on us and thinks he has incriminating evidence. I honestly think the fucker is bluffing, but I'm not

sure" Randall said confused and enraged.

"He's bluffing so don't get all shook up you'll be

fine. The guy is a total waste of space. How he is

still a detective baffles me" I said whimsically.

"Are you sure dude because I'm not able to go to

jail?! I'm not some hardened criminal who raped

or murdered someone. Honestly all we've done

is hacked into people's servers because people

have faulty sites. It isn't our fault that big banks

and businesses have bad security. Thanks to us

they have amped up their security

like mother fucking Fort Knox. We're doing

people a service. Have we reaped financial gain

yes…but we're helping people!

"Dude, Detective Thurston is like Quickdraw

McGraw, he's a flat out idiot. When he was born

and God was handing out brains, he thought he

said trains. Seriously for him to have some sort

of lead is next to impossible. He has had a hard

on for me for years and I don't understand why.

I think we need to give him a reason. I think we

need to do something over the top. I think we

need to extort him once and for all. Do

something over the top. It will land him in jail,

but he will be off our case. How much pain can

you tolerate?" I said with a serious face. I had a

stone face look with the utmost seriousness. My

eyes were as black as coal. I was sick and tired

of fucking with Thurston and this would be the

very last time.

"What do you propose we do? It has to be something huge!" Randall said with eyes almost as big as quarters.

"Well we can go to the bar he likes to frequent and we can get him to beat one us up and draw his gun. All we have to do is use a payphone close by or call with a burner phone" I said with seriousness. I had never been more serious than I was today. Detective Thurston needed to back off and this was the only way. I was sick and tired of him and I felt like he was harassing

me constantly. This would put him behind bars. I

just hope they put him in protective custody.

Prisoners don't like detectives and cops and they

don't last more than a week or two sometimes.

Now all we had to do is follow through with this

plan.

"Ok well who's going to get the beating? Are we

gonna flip for it? He doesn't like either of us, but

he'd be more apt to beat the hell outta you"

Randall said sarcastically.

"Ok well I'll take the beating and you make the anonymous call on the burner phone. We also have to make sure that his lieutenant or someone above him is there. Someone needs to witness it or else he will just be reprimanded to office duty. We also have to make sure he has a large quantity of drugs and a pen drive with something incriminating like important files and a dirty interogation video. Do I make myself clear?" I said sounding excited even though I wasn't. I didn't want to get beat down, but I wanted Thurston out of the picture for good or for a long time. He will probably find out someday it was us, but by then we will probably be in Mexico.

Now we had to plan this interesting feat and we had to do it fast. It's like planning a goddamn wedding in a week. We only had about that to do this in or Thurston would try and find other bullshit on us.

"I'll see what I can do. I have lots of buddies in different places who don't mind getting their hands dirty" said Randall with what sounded like glee. For the first time I could see a gleam in his eye during this whole video chat.

"Ok well over and out until we talk again"

I said to him with seriousness. With that the

video chat was done. Now I had to devise a way

of going to the same place and provoking him. It

wasn't going to be easy, but I knew what pushed

his buttons and it was me.

Chapter 9: A Night To Remember

There she was getting ready to go on her date with Silas. Alex hadn't been on a date in quite a long time. It was 5:00 pm and she was waiting on him like always. She wondered why that really was and she never questioned it. She never did understand what he saw in her either. She wasn't fat or for that matter even ugly. She was fairly pretty and she was what you call thick or chubby. She was proud of her body and she was happy of herself. She wouldn't change her life for anything. She was lucky she met Silas, but she was worried about his reckless lifestyle and she was worried it would come back to bite

him in the ass someday. He may have a good job

in customer support helping people from being

hacked, but he is also a hacker and makes the

bulk of his money maliciously. She really cared

for him though and she really thought that after

only knowing him a month or so that he was

special to her. She was very fond of him and she

felt like saying she loved him or cared for him,

but she was scared to say anything at all. He had

been courting her all this time, but this was the

first time they had been on a big date. They were

going on a date to a fancy restaurant called

Gerard's and she was excited to go. Now she

had to wait until he arrived, even though it

seemed like he had a habit of coming casually

late. She didn't mind because at least he came

and he didn't leave her waiting. She knew he

was busy and she knew that work kept

him busy. She knew his "other job" kept

him busy too and it was something he enjoyed

doing with a group of friends of his. They called

themselves 1_N@t!0n and their mantra was

"United we stand, United we fall". She

wondered who was watching his nephew

tonight. He must have a full time babysitter, but

she never questioned that.

Finally his car had pulled into the

driveway and she was so happy to see his

smiling face. He must have done something

good to be smiling. What he did he might end up

bragging about so she better prepare to hear it.

"Guess what! We were able to hack into

the mainframe of a few of the biggest stores in

the country. We set up a backdoor trojan virus

where we are able to syphon money from their

accounts. We then proceeded to send it to the Cayman Islands. It was a big day for us and I think we need to celebrate. I think we need to buy some expensive wine. Maybe we need to do something out of the ordinary like rent a limo"

"I think we should be as low key as possible Silas. I think your ego is getting the best of you and your suffering from an overload of euphoria" Alex said with as much kindness as she could.

"Ok I see what you mean Alex. I got that s.o.b. Detective Thurston trying to catch me in the act of something criminal. He's trying to dig

up any circumstantial evidence he can on me.

He's quite the douchebag, but he's nothing I

can't handle. I

know that you got my back sweetie. So

did you think about the bank job that we were

thinking about going to do? I think your bank

would be an easy snatch and grab" Silas said

with seriousness.

Alex was taken aback and was thrown a

huge curveball. For a few brief seconds she

thought her heart had stopped. Did he really ask

about it! She thought he was joking. They

mentioned about it on dates or pillow talk, but

she didn't think he was really serious. She had to

think up a lie and quickly. She didn't want him

to think she was stalling.

"Ya sure I can get the passwords and all

the combinations for you. Not a problem. I can

also get all the schedules of when people are

working and everything else. Have you scoped

out the blind-spots? Also you have to be careful

of the guards and you have to be careful not to

get locked in. bringing multiple people and

having a getaway driver is your best plan of action. You also want to take out the cameras by either changing the tape to a loop of the day before or spraying them with spray-paint or breaking them" Alex said apprehensively.

"Ok let's go to dinner I'm getting hungry and you probably are too. We have a reservation and we can't be late" said Silas with a smile.

Alex knew that Silas was trying to fake a smile. She wasn't surprised by it at all. He didn't like to go out and public much at all and she had known since she met him that he was suffering from an addiction to something but she wasn't

she wasn't sure what. He hid it really well and it

seemed like he used only enough to function.

She also knew it wasn't alcohol because he

didn't drink very much. She couldn't pinpoint it

but if she had to guess it was either Oxycodone

or Adderall. She wouldn't be surprised at all, but

she wished he was more careful. She knew he

had his nephew to take care of and he didn't

need to see that.

They finally got to Gerard's and they had

deal with a small snooty French man at the

counter. He was quite the malicious looking prick. He looked like he could wreak havoc on to any individual who messed with him, just with his cold black stare and hairy mustache.

"Do you have a reservation?" the man at the counter asked.

"Yes the reservation should be for Silas Harper at 6:00pm. Please tell me you have it!" Silas said with vigor and a loud voice.

"Yes sir we do have it. We have put you on the terrace like requested. Therefore you can watch the sunset" said the French counter staff.

"Aww how romantic Silas. That is so sweet I can't believe how much planning went into this. You are so nice to me" Alex said with red cheeks.

"It was nothing! It was pretty easy to plan" said Silas.

They were seated on the terrace and they ordered their food. As they waited violinists came by and played for them. If this didn't woo Alex nothing would. Silas felt like he was finally pulling the puppet strings for once. Or was he?

Chapter 10: The Mole

Detective Thurston sat at his desk waiting

as he did some paperwork on other criminals he

was trying to locate. He was waiting on an

informant to come in that had information on

Silas and Randall. This wasn't your ordinary person. This person had inside dirt and knew more than most people. She has been having a relationship with Silas and he was even planning a bank job with her. Her name was Alex and she seemed to be a believable informant. Detective Thurston looked at the clock and noticed it was noon.

"Detective Thurston ummm there's an Alex Upton is here" said his secretary Donna"

"Thank you Donna. Send her in please"
Detective Thurston said with a smile as he
closed his door.

"Hi Alex, Thanks for coming down. How
long have you known Silas? I don't want to here
any bullshit!"

"I have known him a long while. He's a
customer at the bank I work at. I am the head
teller there. We have only been dating 2 months"
said Alex nervously.

"Has he talked about hacking or robberies

or anything illegal to you" Thurston said with a

grin.

"He may have mentioned it, but I don't

really think it's much of mine or anyone else's

business how he makes extra money. As long

he's not killing people or dealing drugs, or

anything that's hurting anyone. Why does it

matter" said Alex aggressively

"You're just a white collar detective with

a hard on. You have nothing on him so you go to

the next closest source and that's me!" said Alex

with rage.

"We can get you for accessory and a list

of other charges. But you can have immunity if

you wear a wire or if you use a recording device

and record him talking. You would need to have

him confess. Think you could do it?"

"Ya I could do it. No problem. I want the

immunity in writing. I'll call you, you don't call

me" Alex said.

"You have one week" said Detective

Thurston.

With that she left abruptly. She couldn't

take anymore bullshit. She had to leave. She

couldn't believe that the police wanted her to be

a mole and the thought of it made her nauseous.

She had a lot to think about. She really loved

Silas and she was worried what would happen to

his nephew. She had a lot to think about and she

didn't have lot of time to think.

Part 2: Ones and Zeros

Chapter 1: 100011

Alex sat in her recliner at home and she started to watch a movie on Netflix. She decided it was a night to spend with herself and a few nice cold glasses of Mimosa. She was sitting there so relaxed that she passed out. When the tiredness hit her she was dead to the world. She started dreaming of all the all the scenarios that could happen if she complied with the FBI and did what they requested. She didn't realize that Silas was in so much trouble and she didn't know what she could do. She asked for immunity in return of a conversation Wearing a wire. She didn't find it nice to have to act like a stool pigeon. If she were to follow suit and help Silas she could be doing time for bank fraud, hacking, identity theft, and a list of other things. She was an accessory to all of Silas's wrongdoings. She didn't want to become some bitch to a butch in prison. She would not be too kosher with that one. She loved Silas, but he wasn't worth going to prison for it. As she thought more and more about it, she knew there had to be a way she could do something about this. She needed a plan and she needed a good one. She had to plan what she was going to do to

down to the buzzer. She would somehow alert
Silas with a note or drawing. She had to do
something because she didn't agree with the FBI
and she knew they would not honor immunity.
They also had nothing on her and that made her
laugh. They wouldn't be able to arrest her. What
if she identified him as Pablo or had someone
else come. It would just be a conversation then.
The FBI would have been listening to nothing
important. She could also break the wire before
they started listening. She didn't care what they
threatened her. They had nothing on her until
they were able to confront him. She knew damn
well they weren't going to give her immunity.

That would be too easy and they still haven't

had an ironclad contract ready to sign. All she

had to do was put the wire into a cup of coffee.

That would probably work just fine. When she

woke up from what was supposed to be a brief

nap, it was already 6:00 pm. She decided to

make a tv dinner and go back to watching tv.

This would be a lot of restless sleep. She had to

pull off the best performance that she would

never have to do again

She called Silas and when there was an

answer, she almost didn't recognize the voice.

"Hey Silas, can you meet me tomorrow at

the park in the pavilion. I really need to talk

about something. I have a plan that will give the

ultimate pay out. Then we can leave to another

country, like Italy" Alex said happily. Had she

just lied to the guy known for lying and conning

people. She felt dirty and putrid for just doing

that. She had a lot to think about before the

initial meet up. This was so mind warping she

even had trouble sleeping.

Chapter 2: Ping

Next morning at 9:00 am Alex woke up more exhausted than she was last night. Alex had to meet with Silas at 10:00 am. She brought an empty coffee cup with the listening device in it. She wished it would have had coffee in it, but Silas wouldn't have a coffee if he showed up with one. It was either now or never and she thought now would be good.

She saw that he had a nice fresh cup of coffee. The listening device was in her empty coffee cup, but it wouldn't be for long. She took the mini recorder and she dropped in his hot coffee.

"You'll thank me later and i'll replace your coffee too. Now let's slowly walk by a trash can and toss it" Alex said nicely in a low voice.

"What the fuck was that Alex? I just got that coffee. I don't know what to expect about that listening device" I said highly agitated.

"You're right it was one and the FBI wants me to turn on you. They have nothing on me, but trumped up charges. They say they have a lot on you though. They would have something incriminating on you if we discussed things we have recently done. I am not going to let them bully me into getting information about you. I decided a long time ago whether I was in it for the long haul or not. Whatever happens will happen to the both of us" Alex said enthusiastically.

"Ok well I admire that and I'm glad you did this, but they will get a hold of you again and when they do, they will want to know why there was no conversation" I said with worry in my voice.

"Don't worry I got this. Do you have that decoy car around here. They know what my car looks like and they know yours too" Alex said

sounding agitated.

"Yes I do and I think letting someone else

use your car might be advisable. I will be ok I

will use my other car. I have a plate changer. My

car has a new plate with the push of the button.

Go to my mom's house and she'll know what to

do. I'll text you the address. Go to the light blue

car by the park pool. It has the last three

characters AZ1. The keys are in the glove box.

The doors are unlocked. Go now!" I said nicely.

"I don't need to do anything else? Just go to the address you texted? Alex said curiously.

"Don't worry about anything else, just get to my mom's house. I am more interested in your safety. She'll know what to do"

Chapter 3: Keygen

Alex searched all over for the car that Silas was referring to. She eventually found it and jumped in, buckled up, and put the keys in.

She punched the gas and she sped off. She knew that the only way she would be safe is if she went into hiding. So she drove over to Silas's moms house and introduced herself. Silas had already called his mom, so she was prepared for the possible fugitive she would be harboring.

Alex arrived to her destination and she parked in the driveway. She was met by Gwendolyn with concern.

"What the hell has he got you tangled in honey. The shit I deal with having a hacker for a son" Gwendolyn said.

"He didn't get me tangled in anything. It was all free will. I did it myself. I just happen to work at a bank he wants to steal from" Alex said vehemently.

"Park the car in the garage smartass and get in here. I'm helping you because Silas asked me to. You also destroyed the listening device, so that shows true character. We don't need snitch drama around here and this place is my home. The FBI will not bully me. You did right by me for not flipping on him. I have a small den off the garage you can hide in. It's fully furnished and has cable and internet. I suggest

you go in there and keep the tv on low"
Gwendolyn said.

"I will check in on you in a few hours. I'll
entertain the dudley do rights" she said
sarcastically.

"Ok thank you Gwen. That is sweet of
you. I will do whatever I can to stay out of
trouble. I think I'm going to take a nap" Alex
said.

"I'll bring some dinner to you when it's
done sweetie. I gotta get back in the house. I fear
your FBI friends will be here soon. She went
back upstairs and sat down. She started a new
crossword, as the tv played classic rock music.

Ten minutes later, as expected, two guys in suits knocked on the door. She got up and answered the door.

"Good afternoon miss, we're looking for your son Silas" said Agent Michaelson.

He was a rather slender guy and he had the face of a weasel. When he talked he sounded like a weasel too.

"Nope I haven't heard from him in weeks. This is his mailing address, but I don't know where the little fucker lives" Gwendolyn said sounding irritated.

"What about his girlfriend Alex. Have you seen her at all" Said detective Thornton. This detective had a face only a mother could love. One eye of his was droopy and he looked like he suffered from stroke face. It was rather funny listening to both of them talk.

"No I haven't talked to her or any of his friends.What the hell did he do now!. Are you retarded in thinking I know any of his friends and associates. Take your fed asses off my porch and leave. In all technicality you are right now you're trespassing. Until you provide me with a search warrant you can fuck off. Good luck with that warrant too because you have no substantial evidence. Good luck getting a judge to sign something this late in the day and you better have some smoking gun evidence" Gwendolyn said with a laugh.

"We'll be back and when we do come back you better let us in. We are not fucking around" said the weasel faced detective. And they drove off angrily. Gwendolyn waved them farewell and walked back in the house.

"You can come out of hiding now. I'll let you know if there is any more issues. I hope everything is good for now and those scumbags don't show back up. You must have pissed them off a lot. What the fuck did you do?" Gwendolyn asked sarcastically.

"Well I destroyed their listening device by drowning it with a cup of coffee. As we walked by a trash can I threw it in the trash" Alex said with a small chuckle.

"You go girl. That takes some real balls to do something like that. Especially if they tried to give you a bullshit deal. Well they will be back for sure then. They think you two are up to something and they will do whatever they can in their power to get you put behind bars" Gwen said sounding worried.

"Don't worry Gwen, they have no real evidence that either of us did anything. Only thing I am accused of is being the lookout. That's considered conspiracy to commit last time i knew. They won't do anything unless they have real evidence" Alex said with a wide grin.

"Don't get cocky little one. The first time you let your guard down is when they will pounce" Gwendolyn said loudly.

"I will watch carefully. I'm hungry did you make anything while I took a nap. I'm so hungry I could eat the ass off a bear" said Alex smiling.

"Do you like meatloaf and fried potatoes? That's what I made for dinner. I even made brownies for dessert" Gwendolyn said nicely.

"Sounds nice. Thank you for your hospitality Gwen. I can tell you really love your son. You're putting yourself at risk too" I said kindly.

"Anything for my son. He's all I have that matters in this world. So you're just like a daughter to me now. Don't fuck that shit up. I don't bring new people into my life easily. Don't break his heart at all. He's a great man with a lot of manners. He has something his father doesn't and that's character" Gwen said sternly.

Chapter 4: Rootkit

"Did you get to my mom's house yet" I asked sounding short of breath.

"Yes Silas. Why what's wrong hun?" Alex asked sounding worried.

"I think they spotted me and the was as chase until someone picked me up off the side of the road and said get in. I'm fine though, I have entrusted my faith with this guy. He must have went through this shit before." I said as my voice cracked.

"Well that sounds like a very noble thing to do. We have to thank this guy somehow"Alex said with a sincere voice.

"Sometimes you make me wonder Alex. I don't think the guy wants cookies for his heroics" I said laughing.

"I like cookies. She can make some chocolate

chip cookies for me if she likes" said Guillermo

trying to be part of the conversation..

"Well tell her yourself then" I said sarcastically.

"Did you get the guys name? What did he look

like?" Alex prodded.

"Yes I did and his name is Guillermo. Maybe

you should jump on that one Alex!" I said with a

hearty laugh.

"A foreign mystery man is not my style. You're enough of a mystery. Ya i just said that." Alex said smugly.

"Well whoever he is, he sure helped us out a bunch. He must not like Feds either. From what I understand, he's a former hacker too" I said with chipper sounding voice.

"I'm glad that you're safe! Be careful though. These Feds are on us like white on rice. I'm not worried yet, but i'm getting to be. None of us are safe" Alex said sounding worried.

"Well I have a few ideas, but it's going to need to involve a password encryptor, a laptop, and a vehicle to get right next to the city police departments WiFi" I said enthusiastically. "Or I will need a disguise and go in as a computer repair guy. I need access to the WiFi to hack it or one of the main computers that's ethernet connected. There are other options too, but they're more complicated. The possibilities with a large magnet are endless too" I continued as I was deep in thought. I was in my own world when I got lost in my thoughts.

"I might have an idea, but it's going to involve a lot of planning. You talked about a magnet, would that completely wipe their servers" Alex said with a devilish grin.

"That's a possibility. It depends on how powerful the magnet. There are a lot of myths about magnets and computers. Everything electronic has some sort of magnets. So the attacking magnet needs to be more powerful than the magnets in the server. Most computers and servers have powerful neodymium magnets. It was a good idea, I like your thinking sometimes Alex" I said with a smile.

Chapter 5: Wipe

I sat there laughing at the insanely clever idea Alex had suggested on the phone. She suggested a junkyard magnet. It might work, but we're talking about wiping data. Unless we're a real threat to national security, our information is on the police department's computer database and local server. The easiest and most effective way to totally kill a hard drive is with heat or water damage. Now it might be risky, but if we set a fire in the building the heat and impending water to follow would destroy everything. I can also find out who their server is managed by and what cloud storage they possibly use. When there's no records on the server of our existence, it will be our word versus the Feds. We could also cut a hole in the roof and flood the entire building. Lastly, we could use a Tesla coil and electrically destroy everything. That is probably the most effective way of killing electronics. Where could I possibly get a Tesla coil though? We might be more successful using a plasma cutter on the rooftop and then flood the place with a hose. Maybe my new friend has some other ideas. It wouldn't hurt to ask would it?

Chapter 6: Destroy

"Guillermo, how would you kill a computer server" I said inquisitively.

"Well the easiest way is to flood or torch the motherfuckin' place. When do you need it done ese? I got a large variety of different people I could hire to do this" Guillermo said with seriousness. The fury and hate in his eyes was serious, and I hadn't even mentioned the target.

"It's the city police department and it needs to be destroyed" I said emphatically.
"I got just the crew for that and they are like ninjas. They are mad expensive though and they

are very thorough" Guillermo said

enthusiastically.

"You have an idea how much these ninjas cost?"

I said with dry humor.

"Probably $100k would be a good guess. Each

person that's on the job breaks it up evenly"

Guillermo said.

"Well get a hold of these ninjas. A job like that

would be worth it. Nothing comes back to me ok

ese" I said trying to be funny.

"I will call them in a few minutes. I can have this done by tomorrow night. They haven't done much the last few months. The criminal side of work hasn't been so lucrative lately. It's much easier to make money doing smash and grab jobs than destructive jobs.

"I hate to sound paranoid, but I have to ask. How did you know I was in trouble and jump in when I needed someone?" I asked with curiosity.

"Do you think my entrance was too convenient? It wasn't meant to be like that. I honestly was only going to the park for a birthday party. I think I had the wrong day. When I was walking to my car, I just happened to see our suit friends, and I knew who they were. They tried to get me to inform on a group of my people. They were accused of robbing a store and a few people who worked in the store said they could identify their eyes and voices. Whether that is actually true is beyond me, I'm not a psychologist, but statistically that sounded impossible. We all sound similar within two octaves and everyone's eyes are similar. Cops play by their own dirty set of rules and have a way of creating bullshit evidence.

Chapter 7: Dark Horse

As I listened to Guillermo talk about his criminal past, I seen some parallels in his story and mine. He was just ungratefully blessed to be born into a minority family. I was born to a white anglo-saxon protestant family. I didn't come from a family of elite or entitled assholes. My family sometimes struggled more than most.

Maybe it was a societal thing or maybe it was a God thing. Either way life really sucked for us. We both had experienced struggle throughout our lives. Look at where we were now. We were planning on making a few big scores and we will change our lives forever. We weren't worried of the ramifications. We were psychopaths who enjoyed the thrill of screwing over people. And we were going to do it too.

Chapter 8: Raspberry Pi

The longer I talked to Guillermo, I realized that pulling off a job was going to take more than one person. We would need to start off fresh, early in the morning.

"Oh hey, we're here! This is my humble abode and i'm in a secluded and secretive place" Guillermo said.

"Awesome, it's perfect to hide out!" I said excitedly.

A good thing to do is secretly install is a raspberry pi. If you haven't heard of one, think of it as a standard circuit board with basic computing functions. It could be controlled remotely once installed. This may be quite the project, but it was well worth it.

My idea is to pose as IT support and when I was fixing the server I could install a raspberry pi. It's function would be to slowly make the servers inoperable. It might just work, but i'm skeptical. I'm unsure of the idea and I decided to keep it in my short term memory and talk to Guillermo later. I might just go with the magnet or a flood.

"So Guillermo, tell me more about your friends and what they can do?" I said inquisitively.

"Well it depends on what you can afford and whatever you want done. If you need it taken care of I got people" Guillermo said in a serious tone. As he said it he appeared to be stone cold serious. His tone slightly changed and his eyes looked darker.

"Ok well I need a building flooded from the top floor down. So I need a crew that has access to a fire truck" I said diligently.

"Or you could cause a fire and then flood the building. Kills two birds with one stone. Don't over-complicate things. I got this bro" said Guillermo with confidence.

"Ok I trust you, but don't let me down" i said hesitantly. I wasn't sure what else to say. I was putting my fate in his hands. My mission for destruction has now also became his.

"Ya I can help you with this and make it go away with 35 G's" Guillermo said confidently.

"I will pay half now and the other half plus extra when it's completed. You think you can do that? I said sternly.

"I got you man! I want to stick it to the police too. They are pissing me off. They never back down like a ruthless doberman. I feel honored to help you.

Chapter 9: Terabytes

Alex sat there wondering what to do next.
She was sitting on the bed; reading her book she
brought with her. The book was "Mein Kampf"
by Adolf Hitler. She wasn't racist or anything
like that, she was just curious. She had watched
"The Man In High Castle" on Amazon. This was
a way to curb her curiosity and bide her time.
She knew they would be back and she would
need to hide. She knew about the small hidden
room that opened with a book. She was willing
to do whatever she could do to avoid more
questioning. They had already lied to her once

and she knew these detectives would lie again. If only she had a way to hack into their network. Who could help her with that though? The only person that came to mind was Silas. She had to think fast. She had heard of a few different sites where you could hire hackers and programmers. It was worth a shot, what did she have to lose?

She found someone on the web named Machiavelli, and after chatting with him she knew he was the perfect choice.

"So after what you have told me, it seems like you need a hacker to destroy some computers or destroy a server! That is a big job, but i'm willing to help" typed Machiavelli. I know of a few very destructive viruses that could do that. Or I could infect their WiFi. What are you willing to pay for a job like this. I charge in bitcoin" he said after a pause.

"How does 15 bitcoin sound. That's about $12,000. Is it worth your wild now" Alex said.

"Yes pay me half now. And the rest when the job is done. Is that ok?" Machiavelli typed hesitantly with a smiley face. "A virus that can infect WiFi is called Chameleon and yes I have a copy on a pen drive. It can literally kill a network" He typed.

"Ok well I need it installed as soon as possibly. A good way to get in is to act as tech support or some sort of professional. Is that a

good idea" typed Alex deviously.

"Yes I can do it. I will not disappoint" He

typed back. And with that it went silent.

Chapter 10: Chameleon

Machiavelli waited intently for the bitcoin transfer to come through and then he would let the games begin. In the note it read: Thank you for the help. I need a virus put into the bank I work at. I want no records and here is the address…"

He knew that bank well. He had helped set up the security in it. They were fairly well locked down, but it was going to be a cinch. At least he hoped it would be an easy smash and grab. He sure wasn't going to tell his new friend

Alex. She wanted no paper trail and he could do that with no problem. She must have been involved in some shady shit. He decided to look her up and found a treasure trove of dirty information. It looked like she was in hiding from being questioned by the FBI. She also had an accomplice named Silas who also was a hacker. He knew Silas personally and he went by the nickname Spark. This was going to be interesting!

Chapter 11: I Am Machine

"Ok team, so we have a mission to destroy all the servers and computers in this federal building. What do you think we should do. I was thinking about setting a fire and put a hose in one of the windows. We have to think fast though. We have a limited window to do this before police will come rushing" said Guillermo authoritively.

"Boss, can't we just flood this place. I'm sure we can put the hose through a window and let it keep it flowing. This will cause electrical issues through the whole building and it's sure to fry everything" said D'artagnan.

"You're a fucking genius Dart. I think you have been just promoted to a full time assistant. See people, it's ingenuity like this that makes us better criminal. Follow him and you will be promoted too" said Guillermo with enthusiasm and excitement.

"Well let's to work then everyone" said Radar. This was Guillermo head assistant in charge of doing missions when he wasn't available. Guillermo had known him since middle school and trusted him with his life. He had a face only

a mother could love with squinty eyes and a

round face with a large scar. He was the larger

one of the entire team, but he could move fast

and lift four times more than everyone. He was

the kind of guy you didn't want to pick a fight

with.

"Don't waste any time and just get it done in an

hour. We are going to make a decent payday.

This is for a new friend of mine. Please don't

fuck it up" said Guillermo politely, but sternly.

"We got this boss. We'll make you proud"said Radar.

"Ya we got this boss" said Hawkeye.

Chapter 12: Petabyte

The mission that Alex gave her hacker friend Machiavelli was genius. She wanted to remove any trace of her transactions and any loans she signed off on. As Alex drifted off into sleep, she knew that all of their lives would change for the better. Each hacker team would score a pretty big payday and so would Guillermo's team.

"Hey Machiavelli what exactly can you do if we need a plan B?" Alex said.

"Don't worry about that honey, I got everything

under control. I know a lot of people in the

darkest of places". I don't think you need to hire

a team, that would be great, but I don't want to

overcharge".

"One more bitcoin i'm is what I'm willing

to pay. You can even clean out any possible

transactions. Use a VPN or something else that

makes you invisible. This is a big necessity

because I don't want any paper trail of any CD's

I signed off on for Silas. Can you do that!

"Yes I can. I will even split any money I

am able to get" Machiavelli said excitedly.

"Ok well I think my work here is done"

said Alex with a devious smile"

Chapter 13: .Exe

Machiavelli sat in his car next to the bank and used his android phone to hack into the banks WiFi. He loaded the app and pressed scan. With that he was able to infiltrate the bank's network. The program generated the password and a default password. This will come in handy later. Now he had to hack into the video cameras. He pressed scan and then infiltrated the cameras. He removed the live feed and made it loop for five minutes at a time.

Machiavelli entered the bank and located the ATM. He made it look like he was doing a transaction by taking $20 out. Then he went to the bathroom and made sure to look around as he was heading back. He avoided any detection from the video cameras by making them loop. No one would ever notice him or properly identify him because he altered his looks. He had a short haircut, he was wearing glasses, neatly shaved, and made himself look like a business person. He wore a casual looking outfit to avoid detection.

He successfully had scoped out all of the doors, hiding spots, blind spots, and got the code that could open the vault. Luckily his client knew the vault codes and the safety codes. He also had to completely wipe the computers and the servers. That would be pretty easy. As he walked by he handed Alex a pen drive with a very destructive virus he told her about earlier. The virus was Chameleon.

Machiavelli left and went to a cyber cafe and searched online where the best place to buy a junkyard magnet. He would use the magnet in the front of the bank and from the back entrance too.. This will work if he was able to avoid detection. He found a shady Junkyard named Millers and dialed the number.

"Hello, this is Miller's and our junk is your treasure. My name is Griff and I'm here to help" said a gruff voice angrily.

"Hey I was wondering if you had any junkyard magnets that you could sell or that I could rent?" Machiavelli said.

"Sure we do, but it's gonna cost you and it will be only for rental. What you do with them is your own choice. It will cost $1000 for each magnet and I would want them back in a day or less.

"Do you accept Bitcoin?" said curiously.

"Ya it's going to cas 2 Bitcoin per magnet and don't fuck me over" said the angry voice. "I know some really violent people who will fuck

you up" he said

With an electrically charged magnet

everything will will be wiped and broken" said

Machiavelli.

Machiavelli said this with a chuckle and a

smile. When they started laughing he looked at

the crew with a serious face. This was their cue

to get to work,

A few minutes later his new junkyard

friend delivered the magnets. He brought them

in a large tractor trailer and honked two times.

"Hey boss our magnets are here" yelled Circuit.

"Don't touch anything you spaz" said Machiavelli.

"Here's your payment as promised I sent it to your bitcoin account.

"Try it out, but make sure you set it at low" said Griff

"Ok boss I started up the magnet". said Circuit. All of a sudden there was a noise Machiavelli will never forget. It was the sound of anything metal pinging into the magnet. This was going to be perfect.

Now he had to figure out how to wipe the bank vault. He finally hacked into the bank's online accounts and sent it all to a Swiss bank account he had. The total that they had from recent transactions was $5 million. This was rather low, but he didn't care. He decided that Alex was going to receive $1 million and he would split the rest with his team.

The next day he decided to talk to Alex and send money into an overseas bank under a different name. This was going to be interesting

"Alex, I wanted to sit down with you and tell you what I decided". He handed her a note and told her what she would receive for a finder's fee. Alex was disappointed at first and then she decided the amount was ok. She wrote on the same paper. Thank you and I am glad you were able to complete this nightmare!"

"No problem at all" said Machiavelli. He then said in writing "If you ever need something else I will be around. Make sure you use a private or a dummy email. Have a great day" he wrote kindly on the napkin. Alex looked toward a table a quick glance away. She needed a refill of her ice tea and she wasn't waiting forever.

"What else do you need hunny. Your date paid for you and said don't worry about the order or the tip" said the waitress whose name Alex

couldn't remember.

 And with that her friend Machiavelli

disappeared into the streets. "What the fuck. He

just left me when ! I had more questions" Alex

said calmly to herself.

Chapter 14: Hard Reset

"Ok so everyone understand what their job is"

said Guillermo with authority.

"I believe we do. Just in case we missed

anything can you repeat our jobs" said Gizmo

confused.

Gizmo was Guillermo's best friend who he grew up with him and they were just like family.

"I will not repeat the job and if I do you will have $1000 taken from your share of the profits. Do I make myself clear!" Guillermo said with authority.

"Ok boss got ya. We don't want to lose our money or our job" said Gizmo with a hard swallow.

"Ok so our mission is to flood the hell out of this building and I don't care how you do it. I will not tell you how or hold your hand. I will only keep watch and assist if needed. Does everyone understand?" said Guillermo.

Chapter 15: Zettabyte

"Hurry the fuck up you little pussies. You're not paid by the hour" shouted Guillermo. "If you idiots want to work for me again, you will get the job done as efficiently as possible" he shouted in a disparaging tone.

"We're working as quickly as we can you moron" shouted Gizmo.

"Oh look someone on the team has a pair of brass balls. Awesome job Gizmo! At least someone is attempting to complete their work as effectively as possible" Guillermo said loudly.

"They could probably learn and complete

a lot more without any verbal abuse" Gizmo said

with rage and fury.

"I think we should keep quiet Giz" said.

"That's some really good advice. I want

this job done tonight" said Guillermo.

"Boss, we have the water flowing into the

building and it's a matter of time before it's

done. Hold your panties you impatient bitch!"

said Gizmo with authority

"Took you long enough didn't it. Watch

out said Guillermo sounding worried"

Guillermo gave a thumbs up and flipped

the crew off. They all ignored it and kept busy.

This was going to be a project that would go down in history. One of the guys tagged the side of the wall with the words "The Nobodies".

Just then, a 45 caliber shredded into Gizmo's shoulder. The pain from the hot bullet engulfed Gizmo's arm like a hit from a jackhammer.

"What the fuck Guillermo! You shot me asshole.

"I'll do it again you rebellious punk. You're luck we're friends, I would have shot you in the head!"

With that everyone went silent and went back to work. No one wanted to get shot and the shot to the arm was what Gizmo needed.

Chapter 16: Kernel

"Ok fucker, my crew and I have finished your job. All the computers and servers have to be damaged. If they're not, they will be dysfunctional at least a few weeks. I see you sent the other half of my money with Ten thousand extra" he said with jubilation.

"I suggest you leave town as soon as possible with a fake ID, some liquid assets, and a brand new identity. I have put two ID's, new

Social Security Cards, passports, and fake birth

certificates for you and your nephew. Consider it

a gift. You can do whatever the fuck you want.

Call me with a payphone or VOIP when you get

to your new destination. I also suggest your girl

goes on the run too. Her history as a crooked

banker will no longer follow. Everything has

been erased and damaged by Machiavelli. Good

luck Silas!" said Guillermo in a normal tone of

voice.

Guillermo was gifted at taking charge and

completing a job and this made me feel more

determined than ever to leave this place. I'm

going to miss this place and all the people I met.

I will not be able to come back for 7 years or

more. By then everything should be cleared up

and I will have escaped extradition. See ya

United States, it's time to check out Mexico I

hear it's nice this time of year.